TO

KATHRYN,

Bill
MELDENHALL

HAYFEST

...It's Not For Everyone

Written by
Ellen Leventhal
Ellen Rothberg

Illustrated by
Bill Megenhardt

For a cow, Sue Ellen had a mind of her own. While the herd strolled to the watering hole in a straight row, Sue Ellen tapped her hoof and imagined dancing at a Hayfest Hoedown. As the other cows grazed in the pasture, Sue Ellen made tiny Hayfest ornaments. And when the sheep and horses drank at the pond, Sue Ellen dreamed joyful Hayfest dreams.

"Sue Ellen, drink up, we're heading back to the barn," said Max, the longhorn.

"I'll be along in a minute," sang Sue Ellen as she gathered grass for a Hayfest necklace.

"I love Hayfest," said Lisa Jean as Sue Ellen hung a necklace around her neck. "But it's not for everyone."

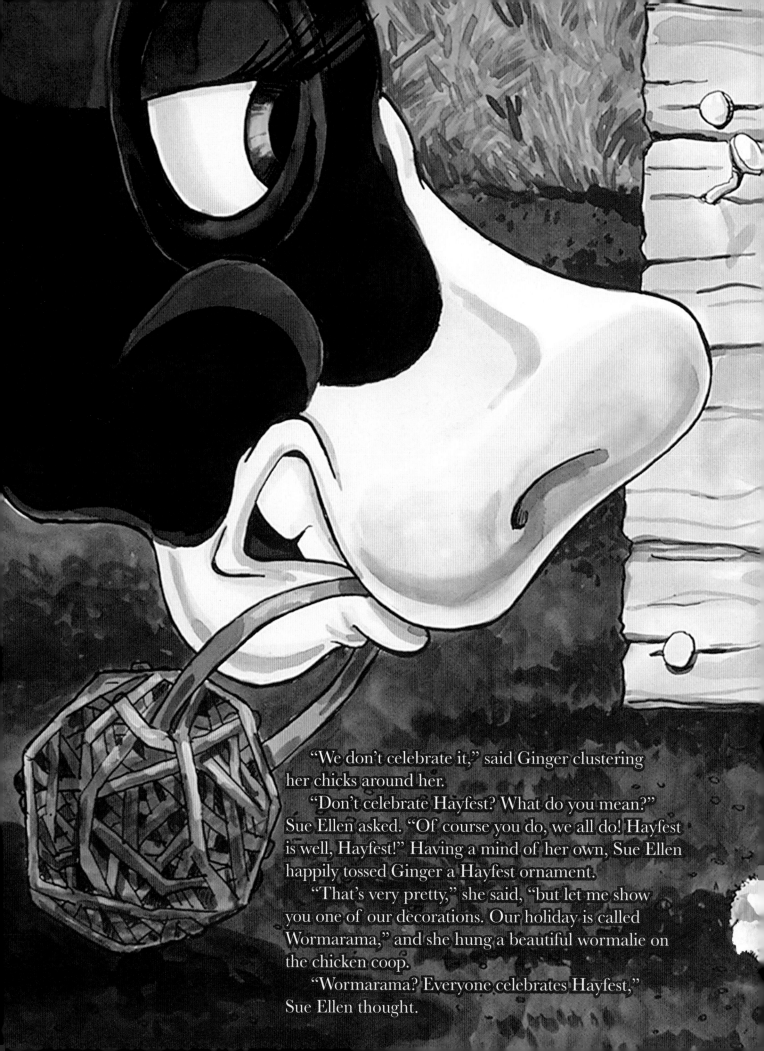

"We don't celebrate it," said Ginger clustering her chicks around her.

"Don't celebrate Hayfest? What do you mean?" Sue Ellen asked. "Of course you do, we all do! Hayfest is well, Hayfest!" Having a mind of her own, Sue Ellen happily tossed Ginger a Hayfest ornament.

"That's very pretty," she said, "but let me show you one of our decorations. Our holiday is called Wormarama," and she hung a beautiful wormalie on the chicken coop.

"Wormarama? Everyone celebrates Hayfest," Sue Ellen thought.

Sue Ellen knocked at the stall of her friend, Gertie. "Gertie, do you need some help getting your hay bale ready for Hayfest?" Sue Ellen called.

"Oh, hi, Sue Ellen," Gertie appeared at the opening of the stall. "No, we don't have a hay bale."

"Why not?" Sue Ellen demanded. "Is it lost?"

"No, we never had a hay bale," said Gertie.

"Of course you have!" shouted Sue Ellen, becoming more and more confused.

"No, Sue Ellen, we don't celebrate Hayfest," said Gertie. "We celebrate Ladybugaloo."

"That can't be," said Sue Ellen, "we've always exchanged presents for Hayfest."

"Of course, that's because we're friends," said Gertie, "but we don't have to celebrate the same holidays."

"Hayfest is fun, but it's not for everyone, Sue Ellen," said Lisa Jean.

On their way back home, they ran into Max. "Max, what do you have on your horns?" Sue Ellen exclaimed.

"Why they're hornaments! It's just about time for Hornzapalooza!" Max answered.

"But there are horns on your horns! That just doesn't make sense! Where are your Hayfest ornaments?" asked Sue Ellen.

"I don't celebrate Hayfest, Sue Ellen," answered Max.

"Wow!" said Sue Ellen. "I can't believe Max doesn't celebrate Hayfest either."
"Hayfest is fun, but it's not for everyone," reminded Lisa Jean.

That evening, Sue Ellen moogled "holidays" on the farm computer.

She couldn't believe what she saw. "Look how many farm holidays there are!" exclaimed Sue Ellen.

Having a mind of her own, Sue Ellen decided to take charge and see for herself which holidays were being celebrated on the farm.

So, Sue Ellen and Lisa Jean
disguised themselves and set off on
their quest.
   They climbed the big oak tree
and spied on the mockingbirds.

They hid behind the hay bales and stared at the horses.

They waded
into the pond
and watched the
dancing ducks.

And finally, they slopped in the mud at the pig pen.

"All this is very interesting, but I don't understand why those animals aren't celebrating Hayfest. Maybe they just don't know how great it is," said Sue Ellen.

So having a mind of her own, Sue Ellen decided to take charge. She gathered her paints and went to work. Then she proudly marched around the farm wearing her sign.

Max saw Sue Ellen's sign and said,
"Moooove that sign out of here, Sue Ellen!
Hayfest is fun, but it's not for everyone!"
    Ralph said, "Oh cock-a-doodle-DON'T
tell me what to celebrate, Sue Ellen! Hayfest
is fun, but it's not for everyone!"
    "Why are they so angry?" Sue Ellen
asked Lisa Jean. " I just want everyone to
celebrate the BEST farm holiday."

"But they like their holidays just as much as we like Hayfest," Lisa Jean answered.

Sue Ellen watched the animals move closer and closer to her sign as each one hung their own holiday treasure.

Sue Ellen looked at her newly decorated sign and pictured Ginger's wormalies on the chicken coop. She thought about all the sounds coming from Max's horns, and she remembered the dancing duck family.

Having a mind of her own, Sue Ellen hooked tails with Lisa Jean and set out to discover the true meaning of the holidays.

"Max, what do you like best about Hornzapalooza?" Sue Ellen asked.

"Why, tooting horns with my nephew, of course. I only get to see him around the holidays," Max said.

DEAR FAMILY & FRIENDS,
THIS PAST YEAR I WAS:
• GRAND CHAMPION
• 1ST PLACE RODEO
• STEER TO WATCH!
Happy Hornzapalooza Uncle Max

Sue Ellen and Lisa Jean strolled past the chicken coop. "Ginger, what's your favorite thing about Wormarama? Sue Ellen asked.

"I like when my chicks sit quietly listening to the story of how the Great Worm got his wiggle," she answered.

Sue Ellen and Lisa Jean walked down to the pond. They asked the ducks what they liked the most about their holiday.

"My whole family swims over, and we do our holiday dance together," answered the mother duck.

"All the families love to be together for their holidays," Sue Ellen said.

"That's what we like, too," said Lisa Jean.

"But I also want the whole farm to be together. I have a great idea, Lisa Jean. Will you help me?" asked Sue Ellen.

"Of course, that's what family is for," Lisa Jean answered.

Soon, all the farm families had their own special invitation.

Celebrate
FARM F

Celebrate
FAMILY
FARM
FEST
DAY!

Celebrate Family
Farm Fest Day!

Worms and bugs,
horns and hay

Come celebrate
your special day

Meet down by
the old oak tree

And celebrate
as a community

The party was in full swing when Lisa Jean said,
"You did a good job, Sue Ellen."

FAMILY
EST DAY

"Well, you know," she said with a smile on her face,

"Hayfest is fun, but it's not for everyone!"

Story Copyright © 2009 by Ellen Leventhal and Ellen Rothberg
Illustration Copyright © 2009 by Bill Megenhardt
The ABC's Press, PO Box 19632, Houston, Texas 77224-9632 phone: 713-937-9184 — fax: 713-896-9887
ISBN: 978-0-9820278-1-3
Ellen Leventhal -- [1951-] — Ellen Rothberg -- [1956-] — Bill Megenhardt -- [1958-]
Hayfest...It's Not for Everyone / Ellen Leventhal and Ellen Rothberg ; illustrated by Bill Megenhardt -- 1st ed.
p.cm.
ISBN# 978-0-9820278-1-3
SUMMARY: Conflict arises in the pasture when the animals don't all celebrate the same holidays. Ages 3-8.
1. Nature -- Juvenile fiction. 2. Holidays -- Junvenile fiction. 3. Team work -- Juvenile fiction. Title
Rita Mills—Book Packaging Consultant—The Book Connection
www.BookConnectionOnline.com

The paper used in this publication meets the requirements of the American National
Standard for Permanence of Paper for Printed Library Materials Z39.48-1984.
Printed in China.